For my siblings—I can always count on you. –H. K.

To all the children on our planet:
hope sun shines forever in your life. –M. A.

Library of Congress Cataloging-in-Publication Data available.

ISBN 978-1-4521-8272-8

Manufactured in China.

Design by Amelia Mack.
Typeset in Tournedot.
The illustrations in this book were rendered in mixed media.

10 9 8 7 6 5 4 3 2 1

Chronicle Books LLC
680 Second Street
San Francisco, California 94107

Chronicle Books—we see things differently. Become part of our community at www.chroniclekids.com.

One Sun and Countless Stars

A Muslim Book of Numbers

by Hena Khan

illustrated by

Mehrdokht Amini

chronicle books·san francisco

One is the morning sun,
a light that slowly spreads.
We hear the first **adhan**
and rise from our warm beds.

Two are hands for making dua
that I join and raise.
I say a prayer from my heart
and offer words of praise.

Three are bags of **sadaqah**,
too heavy for me to lift.
Grandma fills them up for those
who need a helpful gift.

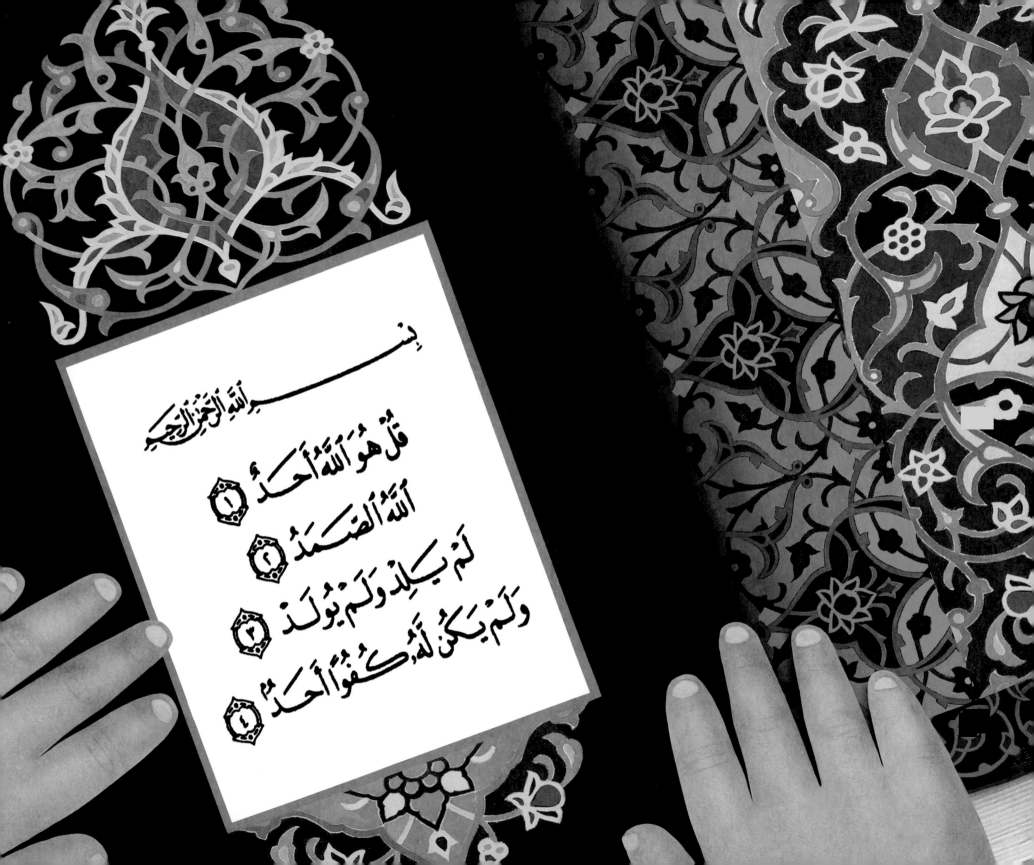

Four are lines of a surah,
one I learned by heart.
Grandpa looks proud when
I recite the whole part.

Five are cups of tea
ready to serve to friends.
    At Mom's weekly halaqa
the learning never ends.

Six are people
traveling by
train, plane, and ship.
They journey to
perform the hajj,
a very holy trip.

Seven are jugs of zamzam,
water cool and clear.
Millions of people drink
this blessed water each year.

Eight are ripe, fresh figs sitting on a pretty plate.
Dad's saving them for **suhoor**, but it will be hard to wait.

Nine are the beads
I count as I say a
special word.
I make tasbih
and know my prayers
will be heard.

Ten are shoes on the carpet,
lined up nice and neat.
When **salah** is over,
we'll slip them on
our feet.

So many blessings in my life,
    like the stars that fill the sky.
I know I'll never count them all,
    but every day I'll try.

Glossary

Adhan (ah-ZHAN): the call to prayer for each of the five daily prayers of Islam.

Dua (DO-ah): a personal prayer or supplication that can be made at any time, separate from required prayers.

Hajj (HAJ): a pilgrimage made to the city of Mecca that every Muslim should perform at least once in their lifetime.

Halaqa (HAL-la-ka): a gathering for the study of Islam and the Quran. It can be informal and held in a home, in a mosque, or anywhere.

Sadaqah (SAD-a-ka): voluntary charity, as compared to the zakat, which is an obligatory charity for every Muslim.

Salah (sa-LAH): the Muslim prayer that is completed at five specific times each day.

Suhoor (su-HOOR): the meal eaten on Muslim fast days, including during Ramadan, before fasting begins at dawn.

Surah (SOO-rah): a chapter of the Quran. There are 114 surahs in total, ranging from 3 verses, or lines, to 286 verses.

Tasbih (tas-BEEH): a form of worship that involves repetition of phrases, often with the help of prayer beads to keep count.

Zamzam (zam-zam): water from a sacred well in Mecca.

Author's Note

There are many significant numbers in Islam. They include one for God, five for the pillars of the religion and the daily prayers, seven for the circles pilgrims walk around the Ka'aba during the hajj, and more.

Mathematics and astronomy were among the intellectual pursuits of early Muslims. They helped to develop algebra and used geometry to create the elaborate patterns found in Islamic art.

For this book, I chose concrete and illustratable terms rather than abstract concepts. The representations for each number focus on tangible things we can count in the world around us.